To my Goodluck family and friend Shirlee and her family,
who all inspired this story with love and humor.
—L. G.

To my family, thank you for giving so much of yourselves
so that I can keep sharing the next creation with you.
—J. N.

Heartdrum is an imprint of HarperCollins Publishers.

Yáadilá!: Good Grief!
Text copyright © 2025 by Laurel Goodluck
Illustrations copyright © 2025 by Jonathan Nelson
All rights reserved. Manufactured in Italy.
Library of Congress Control Number: 2024935608
ISBN 978-0-06-327440-2

The artist used Procreate and Photoshop to create the digital illustrations for this book.
Typography by Rachel Zegar
24 25 26 27 28 RTLO 10 9 8 7 6 5 4 3 2 1

First Edition

YÁADILÁ!

Good Grief!

by **Laurel Goodluck**   illustrated by **Jonathan Nelson**

Heartdrum

An Imprint of HarperCollinsPublishers

HI, I'M HELPFUL NARRATOR, AND I'M GOING TO TEACH YOU HOW TO **YÁADILÁ.**

1. SIT STRAIGHT OR STAND TALL AND PUT YOUR HANDS ON YOUR HIPS OR CROSS YOUR ARMS IN FRONT OF YOU.

2. SHAKE YOUR HEAD SLOWLY, SIDE TO SIDE, WITH A DISAPPOINTED FACE. TRY ROLLING YOUR EYES OR SIGHING DEEPLY. MAYBE SHRUG YOUR SHOULDERS.

3. SAY "YAAA-DUH-LUH" WITH "LUH" PRONOUNCED SHARPER AND A TINY BIT LOUDER.

YAAA-DUH-LUH!

I CAN'T BELIEVE WHAT I AM SEEING!

4. THINK *I CAN'T BELIEVE WHAT I AM SEEING!*

Yaaa-duh-luh!

5. TRY AGAIN. "YAAA-DUH-LUH!" NOW YOU HAVE IT!

OKAY, ALL SET. TURN THE PAGE AND START THIS STORY.

"**Yáadilá!** Dezba! You've been having fun with your dolls all day while we're packing. Come and help. We're almost done," says Dad.

"Ah, I'm going to miss playing here," says Dezba.

Bahe takes Nali's hand as they say goodbye to her home.
Nali whispers, "Hágoónee."
Now Bahe knows she's ready to leave.

"Yáadilá! Bahe and Dezba, settle down.
It's a long way home," says Mom.

"I'll put this in your new room, Nali," says Bahe.

The next morning, Mom says, "Yáadilá! Bahe, don't wake Nali. She was up late unpacking." "Right," Bahe replies.

Later that morning:

"Nali, you're up. What are you looking at?" asks Bahe.

"My sheep camp," Nali says with a deep sigh.

Dezba says, "I want to see, too."

Bahe looks away, thinks for a moment, and then jumps up. "I've got to go."

"Yáadilá! Is that too heavy?" asks Dad.
"Nope, thanks," Bahe replies.

"Yáadilá! That's a lot of twigs," says Dezba.
"I've got a plan," Bahe replies.

"Yáadilá! What are you doing with my scissors?" asks Dezba.
"It's a secret," Bahe replies.

"That's not your room anymore," says Dezba.

"Duh," Bahe replies.

"And you're taking Nali's yarn," says Dezba.

"Quit snooping," Bahe replies.

"**Yáadilá!** Careful with that fresh paint," says Dad.

"I'll clean it up," Bahe replies.

"Yáadilá! Keep out? That's not fair," says Dezba.

"Buzz off," Bahe replies.

Yáadilá! Yáadilá!

"I'm beginning to think that's my name," says Bahe.

"**Yáadilá!** That's my dollhouse," says Dezba.

"I'm just borrowing these," Bahe replies.

"Well, I'm telling. Mom, Dad, Nali!" says Dezba.

"Oh brother," Bahe replies.

At first, everyone is quiet. Then, with glistening eyes,
Mom says, "That's what you've been working on all day."
"That's clearly some good engineering," says Dad.
"Ahh," says Nali.

"Shiyázhí, my little one," Mom whispers in amazement.
"Wow! You did all that?" says Dezba.

Nali says, "It's my summer sheep camp."
"For when you miss home," Bahe says.

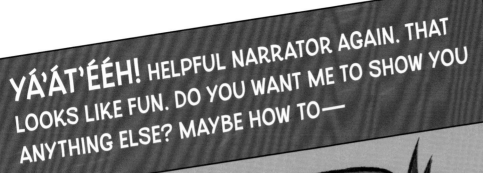

YÁ'ÁT'ÉÉH! HELPFUL NARRATOR AGAIN. THAT LOOKS LIKE FUN. DO YOU WANT ME TO SHOW YOU ANYTHING ELSE? MAYBE HOW TO—ANYTHING ELSE? MAYBE HOW TO—

"Beat it!" exclaims Bahe. "This is my story, not yours!"

HELPFUL NARRATOR'S NOTE

Shhh. Don't tell Bahe, but I'm sneaking back. Wow, wasn't that a fun story?

You learned how to yáadilá. You saw how a little sister could be annoying when you're busy doing something nice for your nali. And how cool was it to learn new Diné words?

Now it's that time in a picture book when you learn about the author. The author—

Excuse me? What are you doing here?

The author has a few words to share on her own. **Yáadilá!** I'm really done. Hágoónee'.

Author's Note

It's nice to finally meet you all. I'm Laurel Goodluck, and I wrote this book.

I come from an intertribal background of Mandan and Hidatsa from North Dakota and Tsimshian from Alaska. I bet you thought I was Diné. Well, *I'm* not, but my husband and two sons are. We all live in Albuquerque, New Mexico. Albuquerque is near the Diné (Navajo) Nation, located in the corners of Arizona, New Mexico, and Utah. It is the

largest Native reservation in the United States, covering 27,673 square miles. I bet you don't know that the Diné Nation is a little bigger than the state of West Virginia. Right? That *is* huge!

I used to run a leadership camp for Native teens across the southwestern United States. It was there that I found the inspiration for this story. My Diné coworker and I led a leadership training session in an outdoor camp setting in the Pecos mountains in New Mexico. My coworker brought her young son and a cousin to care for him at the camp.

I was curious how the child would spend his day while his mom was busy. Well, let me tell you about the fun he had without any toys or books from home. It was hot, so the son and his cousin sat under a shade structure and played with natural items like dirt, water, twigs, rocks, and leaves. Yes, you guessed it: by the end of the day, they had built a miniature sheep camp, complete with hogan, corral, sheep, shade structure, and trails. This really showed a lot of imagination, and I was impressed.

Not only did they build this beautiful creation, but they also incorporated Diné culture while they constructed the sheep camp. The cousin loved her nephew so much, she probably told him Diné stories, sang Diné songs, and used the Diné language to teach him his Diné culture naturally. A lot of Native people teach in this way.

In *Yáadilá!: Good Grief!*, Bahe is growing up with Diné culture in his everyday life, so he knows that creating his nali's summer sheep camp will comfort her.

What is your cultural background? Where is your family from and what culture(s) do you belong to? Do you have special songs, dances, stories, foods, or celebrations? Think of a way that your culture is part of your everyday life. This question may take some thought, and you can talk to your parents, grandparents, or caregivers, too. It's worth exploring, because it is a beautiful part of your life and makes up who you are!

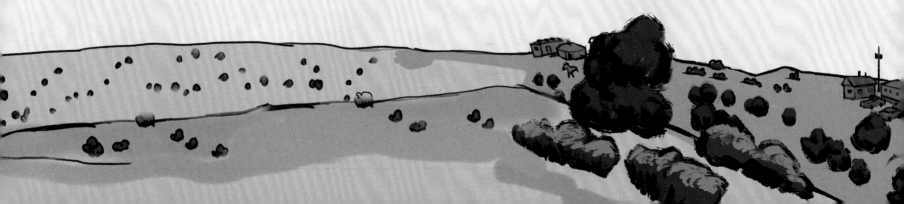

Diné (Navajo) Glossary

Bahe (BAH-hee): the informal form of *Bahí* and the shortened form of the Diné name *Naabaahii*, which means "one who goes to war" or "warrior."

Dezba (Dez-bah): the informal form of the Diné name *Dezbaa*, which also means "one who goes to war" or "warrior."

Hágoónee' (HAH-goh-uh-neh): commonly used in parting to say "goodbye" or "see you later" but also can express the following: "okay," "all right, then," or even "okay, things are settled."

Hogan (hoh-ghun): a traditional Diné (Navajo) home.

Nali (NAH-lee): the informal form of *Nálí* and short for *shinálí* (shi-na-lee), which means "grandma or grandpa on your father's side." In this story, it is the grandma.

Sheep camp: a seasonal home for sheepherding families.

Shiyázhí (she-yah-zhih): "My little one." A common expression that mothers use to convey their love and affection to their sons.

Yáadilá (yaaa-duh-LUH): a common expression used when one is frustrated, upset, surprised, or having a bad day. The expression fits well with the English translations "good grief" or "oh no."

Yá'át'ééh (yah-aht-EH): a common expression for "hello" that literally translates to "it is good" or "all is good."

A Note from Cynthia Leitich Smith,
Author-Curator of Heartdrum

Dear Reader,

Yáadilá! Helpful Narrator could butt in at any moment, so I'm going to talk fast.

Do you hear "yáadilá!" around your home? If so, I bet you're Diné or, like the author, you're from an intertribal family that includes Navajo people. Or maybe the word *yáadilá* is new to you. If so, congratulations! Good job learning a new word. Indigenous peoples like the Diné—or my tribal Nation, the Muscogee—have our own languages, and keeping those languages alive is really important.

Isn't it funny how sometimes the same people who make you want to say "yáadilá!" or "good grief!" can turn around and do something that fills your heart with gratitude? For example, Bahe makes a model of Nali's sheep camp to lift her spirits. How thoughtful!

This picture book is published by Heartdrum, a Native-centered imprint of HarperCollins Children's Books, which focuses on stories about young Native heroes by Indigenous authors and illustrators. I love that we published this book because it's funny and heartfelt and filled with family love.

Mvto,

Cynthia Leitich Smith

In 2014, We Need Diverse Books (WNDB) began as a simple hashtag on Twitter. The social media campaign soon grew into a 501(c)(3) nonprofit with a team that spans the globe. WNDB is supported by a network of writers, illustrators, agents, editors, teachers, librarians, and book lovers, all united under the same goal—to create a world where every child can see themselves in the pages of a book. You can learn more about WNDB programs at www.diversebooks.org.